THE DISCUS THROWER:
A Story of Ancient Greece

D1578714

THE DISCUS THROWER:
A Story of Ancient Greece

By David Oakden

Illustrated by Edward Blake

ANGLIA *young* BOOKS

First published in 1992
by Anglia Young Books
Durhams Farmhouse
Ickleton
Saffron Walden, Essex CB10 1SR

© 1992 David Oakden

Illustrations by Edward Blake

British Library Cataloguing-in-Publication Data

A catalogue record for this book is available from the British Library

ISBN 1 871173 20 5

Typeset in Palatino
and printed in Great Britain by
Redwood Press Limited, Melksham, Wiltshire

AUTHOR'S NOTE

Phidias the Sculptor

Phidias was born the son of Charmides, an Athenian citizen, probably in 490 BC (no firm records exist), the year when the Athenians defeated the Persians at the Battle of Marathon. The wars continued throughout his boyhood, Athens being sacked on several occasions. Phidias began work as a painter, but turned to sculpture and in his twenties made a bronze group at Delphi as a thank-offering for the victory at Marathon. The group showed Athena, Apollo, the Athenian commander Miltiades and Athenian hoplites in armour.

In 450 BC Pericles gave Phidias the task of reconstructing the Acropolis and supervising the erection of the great buildings there. He made a huge statue of Athena, 30 feet high in bronze, armed with helmet, spear, shield and breastplate, which was used as a landmark by ships entering the harbour of Piraeus four miles away. He also made most of the outside decoration for the Parthenon, and inside, in 436 BC, he placed another huge statue to Athena, so tall that the head nearly reached the ceiling. It was carved in wood but with flesh made of ivory and with drapery, helmet and shield made of gold.

In his later life Phidias was accused of embezzling gold intended for his sculptures, but he disproved that charge. He was then said to have tried to make himself equal to the gods by putting a likeness of himself on Athena's shield, and for that he was banished to Olympia. There he made a huge statue to Zeus. He died in 431 BC during the wars between Athens and Sparta.

Little remains of Phidias' work except for fragments of carvings from the Parthenon now in the Acropolis Museum and in the British Museum. However, in 1972 two statues of warriors were brought up from the sea-bed off the toe of Italy. They are made of bronze, hold hoplite shields and spears and one is helmeted. Their teeth are silver, their lips copper, and they probably come from the Delphi memorial to the Greek victory at Marathon, the work of the young Phidias.

CHAPTER ONE

Ari is Bored

Ari was weaving in the upstairs room. Her mother had given her a great deal of work to do, but she was already bored with it. She passed the carved wooden shuttle backwards and forwards through the hanging threads and sighed.

At the other side of the room, the new baby started to cry. Ari got up from her stool and crossed over to the wickerwork cradle. Somebody had left a wooden rattle in the cot and the baby was lying on it, so Ari eased it out and rocked the cradle on its curved wooden stand.

'Hush, baby,' she said. 'Just thank the gods that you are a boy like your big brother Phidias and not a girl like me. Boys can go out and have fun. Girls have to stay in and work.'

Outside, somebody shouted and she crossed to the open window. Below her was a wide, paved street with large houses on either side. This was the part of the city where the wealthy people of Athens lived and at this time in the morning it was very quiet. As she looked a slave came out of a house opposite, blinking in the bright sunlight, carrying a rush basket and going down to the food market for fruit.

Lounging about by a fountain in the shade of some trees, a group of boys had gathered, laughing and talking about going to the river Kifisos for a swim. No girls with them, of course. Girls from families like Ari's weren't even allowed out of the house unless a slave went to look after them.

Ari leaned out and shouted, 'Have you seen my brother?' One of the boys looked up and shook his head, then raced after his friends. A group of old men, dressed in long white tunics and followed by slaves carrying baskets, passed by on their way to the new temple of Athena which was being built on the Acropolis. The old wooden one had been burnt down during the Persian raid some years earlier, and the men were going to make an offering of food and wine. They were followed by a closed litter, carried by four sweating men in loin cloths. Ari could not see who was in the litter, but one of the men was snarling at a puppy which was snapping at his bare heels.

Behind her the baby was still crying. 'Oh, shut up!' shouted Ari. 'We're both prisoners in this house, so just be quiet, can't you? Anyway, where's that slave Naxa? Why isn't she here to look after you?'

Naxa was the baby's nurse and had been bought for the household when Phidias was born. Thinking about her made Ari remember a story the slave had once told, about Ulysses, the famous Greek hero.

She went across and shook the cradle violently. 'Close your eyes,' she hissed, 'or I'll turn you into a piglet, just like Circe did to Ulysses' sailors.' She glanced at her reflection in a polished metal mirror which rested on a stand in the shape of the god Eros. With her long, dark ringlets and short, white tunic, she really did look just like an enchantress. Perhaps if she tried she might manage a little spell or two.

'Sleep, piglet!' she said, raising her arms and swaying as if to witch-like music. 'Sleep, I say. I, Ari, the great weaver of magic, command you. Sleep, or I will make you grow trotters and a curly tail.'

The baby didn't like that. He opened his mouth and yelled so hard that Ari grew really angry. 'Go to sleep!' she shouted. 'Go to sleep or the bogeys will come prowling round in the night and steal you away. And bloodthirsty wolves with dripping jaws will climb through the window to crunch you up!'

'Ari! What are you telling that child?' Naxa the nurse slave came running into the room. 'Let me see him.'

She picked the baby up. The child was wrapped tightly in a long piece of cloth with just his head poking out, so that he looked rather like a butterfly's chrysalis. His face was bright red with howling, but as the nurse rocked him in her arms the noise gradually stopped.

'What a thing to tell your baby brother!' she scolded. 'How could you?'

Ari shrugged. 'It's only what you told me when I was little. When I wanted another story about the old heroes like Theseus, you used to go on about bogeys like Acco and Gello and Gorgo.'

Naxa smiled. 'And did you believe me?' she said. Then, as if remembering something: 'Theseus, did you say? Have you heard the news about him?'

'News? What news?'

'Why, only that our great general, Cimon, has been to Scyros and dug up Theseus's bones and brought them back to bury them here, that's all!'

Ari gasped. 'The bones of Theseus? Was there really a man called Theseus? I thought he was just a hero in a story. Did he really kill the Minotaur? Did he really find his way out of the maze with the help of some thread? Did he really promise to marry Ariadne? Was he really . . . ?'

But Naxa had had enough. She sniffed and took the baby out of the room. 'Too many reallys,' she said as she went, 'and I've got too much on my mind today to bother with you.'

Ari wondered what was upsetting Naxa. Perhaps it was the old trouble again with Theo, one of her father's slaves. Theo had asked her to marry him, but he was a surly and ugly man so she had refused. Ever since then he had gone out of his way to make trouble for her.

Ari was bored. She wandered over to the window again and looked out over Athens. The mountains round the city were misty, but the sun was shining and it would be a bright day. Where she lived the houses were big, with flat roofs and spacious gardens. Further over she could just see the olive trees near the Acropolis, the huge hill in the middle of Athens. On the other side of there, she knew, were the huts and shacks of the poorer people. Then beyond them but out of sight were the long plains leading down to the sea and the port of Piraeus.

A little way to her right the streets were narrow, cobbled or just dirt-tracks and crowded. These were the streets where there were stalls, roofed with skins, selling a huge variety of goods from beaten copper pans to fine linen cloaks. The workers at the stalls, some Athenians, some foreigners, were known as metics but they were all free men and not slaves. Ari could hear them singing and shouting cheerfully.

The nearest of these market streets was the Street of the

Coppersmiths and Ari could hear the rhythmic pant of leather bellows blowing air into furnaces. Down there the flimsy booths and stalls rang with the dint of hammer against metal, and there was the smell of charcoal fires and hot metal.

As she looked, Ari caught sight of a boy, standing in a booth where a furnace glowed and steam rose in clouds. He was tall and sturdy with short, fair hair which curled over his ears and his tunic was grubby, as if he had wiped filthy hands on it. As he bent to pump the leather bellows, he turned his face up to wipe sweat from it, and Ari recognised him. She almost shouted out in astonishment, for it was her brother, Phidias. But what was he doing down there, working like a common market-trader?

She had to find out, so she decided to risk sneaking out of the house. She tiptoed to the door and listened, but the house seemed quiet and there was nobody to stop her, so she slipped on her leather sandals, tied a rope girdle round her waist and ran down the stairs into the street. There were a lot of people about, but Ari dodged round them and made her way through a maze of open stalls until she came to her brother.

The booth was noisy and smelt of hot metal. A round pot full of a red-hot liquid metal glowed and smoked among the coals of the furnace, and the walls were hung with strange iron tools. Phidias was helping the smith, an old but brawny man with a full grey beard. They were standing on either side of a rough clay mould on the sandy floor, and just as Ari arrived the smith struck it a blow with a short hammer. The clay split open like a nut-shell and out˙fell a small bronze figure, glowing red with heat.

'There!' said the smith triumphantly as he straightened his back. 'That's it, at last!' He picked the little statue up in a pair of long iron tongs and plunged it into a tub of water. Clouds of steam rose into the air, making Ari jerk backwards in fear at the dreadful hissing sound, but Phidias leaned forward eagerly to look. As the statue came dripping out of the water Ari saw that it was of a soldier, holding in one hand a round Greek shield, and in the other a throwing spear.

The smith turned to Phidias and said, 'There, young sir. There he is. One of our soldiers from the Battle of Marathon where we beat the mighty army of Darius the Persian. What do you think of him?'

Phidias shook his head. 'It's all right, Solon,' he said politely. 'In fact, it's one of the best I have seen. But you have not got the movement of the shoulder right. See. When an athlete throws a javelin, his arm goes so.' The boy took up the position of a javelin-thrower, body arched backwards and arm extended. He straightened up again. 'If only I could try to make one, I'd do it better, I'm sure.'

Solon roared with laughter. 'Well done, young sir,' he grinned. 'You're right, of course. This isn't perfect, but then I am only an ignorant smith so what do I know of throwing javelins? All that I know is that I have to make several of these every day to make a living. I haven't got the time to get things exactly right, but then the people who buy them aren't experts either.'

'Why do they buy them then?' said Phidias.

'Oh, they just want something to remind them of our glorious victory at Marathon. And don't forget that next year is Olympic Games year, so everybody in Athens will want to buy likenesses of athletes.'

He rubbed a few grains of sand off the little statue. 'As I said,' he grinned. 'I am only a poor craftsman. But, you, young Phidias, when you are a man and have become a famous sculptor, you will make fine statues. I shall remember then how you put me right in this market!'

He reached behind him. 'Here,' he said, 'take this. It's one of the discus throwers you watched me make the other day. Have a look at it and tell me what mistakes I made with that one.'

Ari thought the smith was making fun of her brother, for she couldn't see anything wrong with the figure. She would have liked it for her bedroom to frighten away the bogeys. Phidias flushed but then he laughed. 'All right, just wait and see,' he said, 'but it's good of you to teach me. I'll be back tomorrow.'

Saying farewell, he grabbed Ari's arm and took her away. 'What are you doing here?' he said crossly. 'This is no place for a girl on her own. Where is your street-slave? Father will be furious.'

'I could say the same to you,' said Ari with a sly grin. 'Does Father know that you are learning how to cast bronze statues? He would be delighted to think that his oldest child, son of one of Athens' most famous citizens, was learning how to be a market tradesman!'

Phidias flushed. 'Listen,' he said. 'You'd better not say anything or I might suggest to him that he ought to keep you locked in the house.' Then when Ari was about to speak, he went on, 'In any case I am not going to be a tradesman. I am going to be a sculptor, so famous that my statues will be in every public building. One day this city will be the finest in the world and I shall be known as Phidias the great sculptor.'

'Phidias the modest sculptor,' mocked Ari.

By this time they were back at the house. Ari was about to go in, but Phidias caught her again by the arm, hissing, 'You won't tell Father? Promise?'

'Let go. You're hurting me,' said Ari.

'Promise!'

'Oh, all right. You go and do your silly metalwork, but it's not fair. All I can do is stay about the house. I want to do something exciting too.'

'Such as?' said her brother.

'Such as going to the Gymnasium and joining in with the boys and men. I want to race and throw things like you do.'

'Throw things?' said Phidias sarcastically. 'It's not just a matter of throwing things. It's skill, and training and it's only for boys. Girls can't go.'

'Why not?'

'Because they never do. Girls never take part. You can watch the games when we perform in public, but you can't join in and you can't watch us training.'

'I don't see why not.'

'Well, for one thing everybody is naked, and it would not be right for a young girl to be there. Anyway, girls just don't go, so that's the end of that.'

Ari was about to start arguing with him when a tall man in a heavy cloth tunic and cloak came out of the door. This was Charmides, their father, on his way to the Senate, where all citizens had the right to meet to make laws and to govern the city. He was rich, well respected in Athens and highly thought of as a clever politician. He eased his cloak over his shoulders and looked down at the children. The slave called Theo, the one who had upset Naxa, was with him.

'Well,' he said. 'What are you two up to? Is there no school? Ari, I hope you have not been out on your own.'

Phidias spoke quickly and respectfully. 'Good morning, Father. We've been for a stroll in the market. There is no school today, but the master has told the boys to go to the Gymnasium to practise for the City Games next month.'

Charmides nodded. He liked the thought of his son becoming an athlete and appearing in the great stadium while the whole of Athens watched. Perhaps in five years' time, after his army service, Phidias might even become an Olympic athlete, rich and famous, admired by all. He smiled and turned to Ari. 'And you, little mouse? No learning of books today? Do I not pay Naxa to teach you?'

Ari nodded vigorously. 'She teaches me,' she said. 'She tells me stories about the one-eyed giant called Polyphemus, and about Perseus and the Golden Fleece, and about Circe who turned sailors into pigs. I like that story very much. But today Naxa has to look after the new baby, and she is also worrying about her sister's child who is dying, she says, because the house is damp and he has fever.'

Charmides frowned. 'Hm. Your mother said she'd been a bit odd recently. Did you know about this, Theo?'

The slave scowled. 'It's all lies, master,' he said. 'She is not a good worker. You ought to sell her and get a better nurse.'

Ari opened her mouth to protest, but her father said, 'That's none of your business, Theo. Here, take this money and go to the market. Buy some fruit and take it to the sister.'

He turned back to the children. 'If it is true, Naxa should have said. I know her sister well because she too was a slave here at one time. 300 drachmas she cost me. I released her to marry some foreigner who then went and got badly injured in an accident at the docks. She was a really bad bargain.'

He gathered up his cloak and walked away, leaving the two youngsters to go into the house, thankful to have got away without being found out.

As they went in, Phidias said, 'Keep my secret.'

Ari ran up the stairs shouting, 'Have a good time at the Gymnasium.' But as she went, an idea was churning round in her mind. That morning she had managed to get out of the house without being seen. Naxa the slave was acting a little strangely, and in any case would be busy with the baby. With a bit of luck she would be able to slip out again that afternoon, and if she did she knew just where she would go and what she wanted to see.

CHAPTER TWO

Ari Has an Idea

An hour later, Phidias was in the Gymnasium, an open-air square with a sandy floor and a high wall round it. He had left his clothes in the covered changing-rooms and was with a group of other boys, warming-up. They were under the guidance of an oldish man named Crassus, who wore a long, purple cloak and held a forked stick.

The boys, naked and oiled, sweated through a set of exercises to music played on lute and harp. Six or seven monitors, assistants to Crassus, worked with the boys, correcting movements, giving encouragement and urging on the lazy or tired.

Phidias had enjoyed a plunge into the cold fountain before work began. But after that, while slaves oiled and sanded him, he had started to think again about how one day he would be a famous sculptor. He did not want to be an athlete so this training was all a waste of time.

Soon the group work ended and they were told to carry on with individual practice. Phidias was getting to be an expert at throwing discus and javelin, but today his heart was not in it. He idly made a few throws, nowhere near his best, and then sat down on a stone bench, thinking about the figure which Solon had cast and trying to work out why it looked wrong.

He was roused by a sharp thrust from a forked stick.

'Get up!' said Crassus. 'Work, boy. What's the matter with you?'

Phidias sighed and stood up slowly. Crassus said, 'Look at your friend Lampros. See how he works.'

Lampros was getting ready to throw a javelin and as he watched Phidias stiffened with excitement. He saw the way the muscles moved as his friend bent and hurled the spear and suddenly he knew what was wrong with the bronze statue which Solon had made. It was obvious now. Solon just had not studied how a man's body works. What a real sculptor had to do was to watch and learn about movement and muscles, because only in that way would he be able to show the true shape of an athlete in action. That was the difference between an artist and a craftsman.

His mind churning, he went over to the discus area and worked really hard for twenty minutes, by which time he felt that he had done enough.

'One more throw,' Crassus shouted.

Phidias picked up the metal disc, weighed it in his hand, swung round with it smoothly and gave a mighty heave so that it flew up towards the sun, skimming over the arena and landing at last in a spray of sand. A ripple of applause went up, for it had been a magnificent throw, one for the records. Clapping came from everywhere, and even when it stopped, one person still carried on. Phidias looked round. The clapping was coming from the top of the high wall surrounding the Gymnasium. He shaded his eyes to see who it was.

There was somebody up there, small, dark-haired and dressed in a short tunic. Whoever it was had a loud, shrill voice, for suddenly, through cupped hands these words rang all over the gymnnasium: 'Good throw Phidias!

Well done! But why can't girls join in?' Then in a really loud shriek: 'I am the mighty Circe and people who won't let girls throw things are just pigs. So pigs you shall be!'

The little figure raised its arms as if to cast a spell, but a roar of anger came from Crassus. 'It's a girl!' he shouted. Two of the monitors headed for the wall, but the figure disappeared quickly.

'Who was it?' Crassus asked. 'Did anyone see? Some slave child, I'll be bound. I'll have her whipped.'

The monitors did not catch the girl and nobody seemed to know who she was. Phidias kept quiet, for nothing would make him say that the watcher on the wall was someone he knew well, Ari his sister. He went to the dressing rooms where he used a metal comb to scrape his skin free of dust, oil and sweat and then, shouting a farewell to his friends, he dressed quickly and hurried off home.

As he reached the house he looked up towards the upstairs windows. Somebody was waving at him and shouting something. Phidias shook his fist, because he could see that it was Ari, though her words were lost in the noise of the street.

'I'll get you!' yelled Phidias, but as he made for the door another figure in a dark cloak rushed past him, nearly knocking him flying. He staggered and caught the edge of the wall to steady himself, but before he could say anything, the figure had gone, down the street and out of sight.

'Hey!' yelled Phidias, then looked up again as he heard Ari shout, 'Why didn't you stop her?'

When Phidias got upstairs Ari was standing in the middle of the room, holding the baby. 'What's going on?' he said. 'Why have you got the baby? Where's Naxa and who was that idiot who nearly knocked me over?'

'That was Naxa,' said Ari, her eyes wide with excitement. 'She was crying and saying that Theo told her she was going to be sold. Now she's run away, and what's more she had her arms full of meat and bread she'd stolen from the kitchen.'

'Then she'll be caught,' said Phidias. 'And when she is, she'll be put in chains and whipped. She'll certainly be sold and she might even be branded. Serve her right, too. The law of Athens has no pity on runaway slaves and thieves.'

'How can you say that about someone who cared for you when you were a baby?' said Ari. 'Anyway, I can guess where she's gone. She's gone to the house of that sister who has the sick child. I bet that's why she stole food as well.'

She would have said more, but at that moment their father came in, followed by their mother. She was tall, white-robed and had her hair done up in an elaborate but beautiful style. Going over to the cradle she picked up the baby and comforted him.

'Take the child out of here, Hebe,' said Charmides. 'I can't stand all this crying.'

He turned to the children. 'Well?' he said. 'Where is the

16

slave Naxa and why is she neglecting the baby? Perhaps Theo is right and I should get rid of her.'

Ari began to stammer out some story, but Phidias said, 'Naxa is not here.'

'Not here?' said Charmides. 'Where is she? What have you done to her?'

Phidias went red. 'Don't blame me,' he said. 'I haven't seen her all day, not since I went out first thing to help Solon in the market.' His voice tailed off as he realised what he was saying.

Charmides narrowed his eyes. 'Solon? The market? What's this?'

Phidias could not lie to his father. Slowly at first, but then more enthusiastically, he told him how he was learning from the smith, how he knew that he could do better figures than the market craftsmen and how one day he intended to make a great statue to the goddess Athena.

'One day, Father,' he said proudly, 'the whole world will come to Athens to see the works of Phidias the Sculptor.'

Charmides snorted with anger. 'Sculptor? Rubbish. No son of mine is going to soil his hands making tawdry souvenirs for gawping visitors. You're going to be a statesman and take a noble part in running this city. Leave the donkey work to those with no brains.'

'But . . .' began Phidias.

'No buts,' roared his father. 'You will do as you're told. And what about you, miss? I suppose you want to be something stupid, too?'

Ari said. 'Oh, no, father. I just want to be an Olympic athlete and go to train with the boys.'

Charmides went pale with anger. 'How is it that I have reared two such idiots?' he said. 'And I can still hear that baby crying down below. Where is that slave?'

Without thinking, Phidias blurted out the story of Naxa's disappearance.

'What? Is that the thanks I get for sending fruit to her sister?' roared his father. 'Theo was right about her. I'll send him to find her. He can go first thing in the morning, and he needn't bring her back here because he can take her straight down to the slave market to get rid of her.' And he stormed out of the room.

Ari rounded on her brother. 'Why did you have to tell?' she said. 'Naxa is like a friend to me.'

Phidias said, 'She's only a slave.'

Ari said, 'Even a slave can be like a friend when you're stuck in the house all day like I am with nobody else to talk to.'

Phidias shrugged. 'You spoil her. But Mother does need her. Perhaps she would help if we told her what Theo said.'

'Mother won't dare to go against Father's wishes,' said Ari. 'But if I could get Naxa to come back here of her own free will, she might stand a chance. Father's not as cruel as he tries to make out, and if he could just see her and listen to her, I'm sure he would let her stay.'

'She won't risk coming back here,' said Phidias.

'Oh yes she will, because I'm going after her.'

'Going after her?' said Phidias. 'Don't talk nonsense.'

But Ari was determined. 'I have to find her before Theo gets to her,' she said. 'He won't show any mercy. He'll put her in chains and sell her to the cruellest man he can find. If I know him, he'll go before it gets light, so I must get there first and persuade her to give herself up.'

Phidias shook his head. 'You can't go on your own,' he said.

Ari said, 'I can. I know where her sister lives, in the old town, on the south side of the Acropolis. When everyone's asleep tonight, I shall go to her.'

Phidias knew she meant it and wondered what to do.

'Well?' she said. 'I suppose you'll go and tell Father now and get him to stop me.'

Phidias made his mind up. 'No,' he said. 'But now you've told me what you're going to do, I shall have to come as well. Think what Father would do to me if there was trouble and I'd let you go out on your own. After all I'm a man and you're only a girl.'

'Oh, thanks,' said Ari. 'It's good to know what you think of girls. And I'm glad to see that you think more of your own skin than of my safety. But I don't want to get you into trouble, so I'll let you come. Of course, it would be better if the goddess Athena came, even if she is a woman, but you'll be better than nothing.'

'Don't mock the gods,' said Phidias quickly. 'Remember

that on Athena's shield hangs the head of the gorgon Medusa, which can turn people to stone with its gaze. You'd make a fine stone statue, finer even than any I could make. Just be careful what you say because you never know when she might be near.'

At that moment there was a whirr of wings outside the window and an owl shrieked. Ari went pale. 'An owl!' she said, shivering. 'People say that she takes the shape of an owl. Oh, Phidias, I'm scared.'

She sank to her knees. 'Mighty goddess Athena, please don't be angry. I need your help.'

But Phidias was now excited. 'Don't you see?' he said. 'If that is the goddess, she's letting us know that she is on our side and is nearby to help. It's a good omen.'

He looked out of the window. The sun was setting over the hills and a white mist was creeping across the fields. Lights were beginning to flicker and the streets near their house had gone quiet. Then as he looked the owl came back again, flying low, a white blur in the gathering twilight.

As he watched Phidias whispered, 'Is that really you, Athena? Help us tonight and I will raise such a statue to you that men will come from all over the world to marvel at it. And I shall place it there, on the Acropolis.'

From far away came a faint shriek as the owl dropped like a stone on to some creature below. Phidias closed the window and went to bed.

CHAPTER THREE

The Blue Dolphin

Darkness fell swiftly over Athens and a half-moon was riding high above the scudding clouds, when a wooden window shutter in a small store-room at the house of Charmides was slowly pulled open. A cool wind slid into the room and somewhere down the street a dog howled.

'Hurry up,' whispered Ari impatiently as Phidias tried to squeeze his bulky body through the small opening.

'This window is so small,' said Phidias. 'Hold my legs while I go out head-first.'

Ari's spinning wheel was in the room and she pushed it out of the way, tangling herself up as she did so in the skein of wool she had spun earlier. Crossly she pulled it off the wheel and stuffed it in her tunic. Meanwhile Phidias had squeezed his hips through and was feeling above him for the roof-tiles. His fingers caught on a wooden beam, and he smiled. Now it would be easy. Grasping the beam, he swung his legs out, hung for a second and dropped silently on to the roof of a low shed.

He pulled his tunic down and felt for a little leather bag on his belt, in which was the figure of the discus thrower, brought along as a good luck token. He patted it and looked up at Ari's face peering down at him out of the window. 'Come on,' he said. 'It's not far to drop.'

Ari was smaller so was able to slide out feet-first, landing in a heap near her brother. Seconds later they were both in the street.

'Right,' said Phidias. 'Which way?'

Ari said, 'It all looks different in the dark, doesn't it? But Naxa has often said that her sister's house is to the south of the city, where the freed slaves and tradesmen live, on the other side of the Acropolis.'

'The south of the city?' said Phidias. 'We stand no chance of finding her if that's all we've got to go on. I went down there once, and it's a great mass of shacks and huts, hundreds of them.'

'It's quite close to the olive groves at the foot of the Acropolis. Oh, and the door has got a dolphin painted on it,' said Ari. 'Her brother painted it, a blue dolphin leaping out of the water. She's often told me about it.'

Phidias nodded. He remembered now that Naxa had told him, too, of the beautiful painting of the dolphin, the only one of its kind in the city, she had said.

'Well, let's hope we can find it,' he said. 'Near the olive groves, you say? Right, follow me.'

Ari was about to say that she didn't see why she had to be the one who did the following, but really she was glad to let her brother go first. There would be time later on to remind him that girls were as good as boys at some things.

It was quiet as they made their way towards the mass of the Acropolis, the huge hill which overshadowed Athens. On the west side, where they lived, the slope to the summit was gentle, but by the time they had worked their way round to the south, rugged cliffs rose for hundreds of feet, almost blotting out the light of the half-moon.

22

Down there the road led through rough grassland and then olive groves. Many of the trees were broken and burned and Ari and Phidias found themselves stumbling through piles of rubble and pieces of timber blackened by fire. 'The Persians,' said Phidias. 'When they sacked the city a year or two ago they burned down the old wooden walls. But now men are rebuilding, flattening out the top of the Acropolis and filling in the fissures and caves. There is talk of a beautiful new temple to Athena.'

'Athena should be here with us now,' grumbled Ari. 'She might be able to stop me stubbing my toes on these rocks. Can you see where we are?'

Phidias took her arm. 'Have courage,' he said. 'Look, here are some houses, so if what you said was true, Naxa's sister must live close by.'

They left the olive trees for a narrow street between houses. It was unpaved and down one side ran an evil-smelling stream.

'Pooh!' said Ari, picking her way through a muddy patch and holding her nose in disgust. 'Look at the state of my sandals. How can people live in such a foul smell?'

Phidias said, 'It's not their fault. There are no drains and the houses are just shacks. Look, some of them have no doors, just sacks over the opening. Keep close to me.'

The street led on downwards and the two looked closely at each door as they passed, searching for a painted dolphin. Once they had to dodge into the shadows as a party of drunken men came shouting and singing, on their way home after a bout of drinking. Once rats scurried out of their way when Phidias stumbled over a broken wooden doorstep.

'I don't like this place,' said Ari. 'Everywhere smells of smoke.'

In fact the street they were in was full of drifting smoke, coming out of doorways and holes in the rough walls and roofs.

'Their fires are still in,' said Phidias. 'Or perhaps they are already stirring, getting ready to work when daylight comes. We must hurry.'

They turned a corner and Ari squeaked with dismay as she put her foot in a foul, green and slimy puddle. But Phidias caught her sleeve. 'Look,' he hissed. 'The house with the blue dolphin.'

The house was more like a shack made of odd pieces of wood and rough plaster. From a hole in the flat roof a faint wisp of blue wood-smoke curled downwards to the street, and there, on the door, was a faded painting of a blue dolphin, leaping out of white waves in a cloud of spray.

'That's it,' said Ari and ran to the doorway.

'Wait!' shouted Phidias. He started forward, but as he did so a rough hand closed over his mouth and he was half-pushed, half-carried into the house, where he found himself sprawling on the mud floor, straining his eyes to see.

CHAPTER FOUR

The Chase

An oil lamp gave off a flickering light as Phidias struggled to his feet and looked round. Nearby, on the floor, was Ari, choking from the smoke and rubbing at her eyes, while bending over her was Naxa the slave. Naxa was shivering with fear and her eyes were red from crying. Then, as his eyes got used to the darkness, he made out another woman, lying on bed-rugs, holding a child. There was no furniture apart from two rough wooden stools and a box with a lid on which were the lamp, a two-handled jug and a small piece of bread.

The man who had carried Phidias in stood with a club in his hand, his back to the door. He had a black beard and under his short tunic one of his legs was withered and bent.

'Why? What?' stammered Phidias.

'Quiet,' said the man, speaking with a foreign accent. 'Why have you brought danger here? Who are you?'

Naxa looked up. 'They are Charmides' children, Zeno,' she said. 'They must have come after me.' She turned to Phidias. 'Why did you come? Have you led your father here? Are his slaves ready to take me back and beat me?'

Ari said, 'That's not fair. We came to warn you. Father has told Theo to come here in the morning and take you to the slave market. But listen, if you return with us now and give yourself up, we'll ask Mother to help.

Naxa rubbed at the tears in her eyes and said, 'Your

mother is kind, but your father will believe Theo not me, and that man hates me. I shall be beaten, and branded and sold.'

Phidias said, 'I'm sure if you go back now, Father won't do that. You've been with the family too long.'

Ari said, 'Phidias is right. You risk everything by staying here, and your sister and her husband are also at risk for helping a runaway slave. Come back, do. Our father would be merciful. Did he not send fruit here?'

'Fruit?' said Naxa. 'We have seen no fruit.'

'Theo! He must have kept the money,' said Phidias.

'How bad is the sickness?' asked Ari, looking at the pale face of the child, who seemed to be sleeping in his mother's arms. 'Is he going to die?'

The mother started to sob quietly. 'Hush, Pomponia,' said Naxa soothingly to her. 'No, the worst is past. The food I brought has saved them, I think. Tomorrow Zeno will be able to go back to work, and then all will be well. When you arrived I was just about to leave to go down to the docks and see if I could persuade a ship to take me away from Athens for ever.'

Ari said, 'No, don't do that. Please just come back. But do it quickly, because Theo . . .'

She was interrupted by Zeno who gave a warning hiss, gesturing at them to be quiet. From outside came the sound of running footsteps. They stopped and a low voice said, 'There. Look. The blue dolphin. Wait till I catch my breath.'

Naxa went white. 'Oh, no!' she whispered. 'We shall all be punished. Let me run so that they follow, then the rest may be saved.' She started for the door, but Phidias was before her.

'Stop!' he hissed. 'We can fool them yet. Theo's not too bright. Listen, Ari and I will lead them away but if we do that for you, you must promise to go home and seek mercy from our parents. Promise!'

Naxa hesitated, but then nodded her head.

Phidias went to the door. 'Ari. Put Naxa's scarf over your head and then just do what I do.'

They listened and heard a man whisper, 'Right. I'm ready now. We'll rush the door and take them by surprise.'

'Ready?' said Phidias. Ari nodded.

'No, stop,' hissed Zeno. 'It's too dangerous.' But at that moment, the baby gave a faint cry.

'Now!' shouted the man outside.

'Now!' said Phidias, and they burst out of the door, scattering the three men who stood there and bolted off down the street. 'Run, Naxa!' he shouted and Ari called out, 'Wait for me, Zeno. Wait!'

Within seconds they were round a corner and running at top speed, Phidias calling out from time to time, 'Run, Naxa, Run!'

Footsteps sounded behind them and Ari glanced over

her shoulder. Three dark figures were just in sight, running after them and shouting.

'Make for the olive groves,' panted Phidias. 'That will give Naxa time to get out of the house.'

They ran on, but it was uphill now and the footsteps behind were gaining. They heard one of the men shouting that he could see them, then the dark shadow of the Acropolis towered ahead, and at last they were in the trees. Phidias caught Ari's hand and panted, 'They're too close. Make for the cliff face. I noticed some wide cracks and we still might keep them guessing.'

For a time the trees sheltered them, but then suddenly they were stumbling through loose rocks below the cliff face. Behind them they heard Theo shout, 'Got them! You can slow down. There's no escape now.'

But Phidias was climbing, urging Ari to follow him. A deep fissure ran in the smooth rock, dripping water and as slippery as ice, but wide enough for them to find handholds on both sides. Panting with fear, they climbed on until at fifty feet the fissure widened into a cave entrance. There they paused and looked down. In the pale light of the half-moon they could see the men looking up.

'We can wait!' Theo called. Then they heard another man say, 'Are you sure that's Naxa? I thought she was taller than that.'

The moon came out from behind a cloud and Ari pressed back into the shadows. 'Why do you want to hurt me?' she called, imitating Naxa's rough accent. 'Go and tell Charmides that I am coming back.'

'See, that's Naxa, all right,' said Theo. 'Come on, Naxa. Come down. We only want to give you what you deserve.'

The three laughed and Ari shivered. She had heard of slaves who were beaten until they were never able to walk again, then branded with red-hot irons so that everyone knew that they had once tried to run away.

'You'll never catch me,' she called. 'I'd rather stay here than face a beating.'

One of the men said again, 'Are you sure that's Naxa? That didn't sound like her. It was more like . . . I don't know, but I'm sure I know that voice, and it isn't Naxa's.'

'Rubbish,' said Theo. 'But we'll settle it. Let's climb up and pull 'em down. I owe that woman a beating.'

Phidias said, 'Quick, in here.' He grabbed Ari by the hand and they squeezed into the cave opening. It was narrow and dark, tall stalactites hung down from the dripping limestone roof and they felt loose rocks at their feet.

'Is it safe?' said Ari as she helped Phidias to heave a large rock to one side, but even as they squeezed past it there was a heavy rumbling noise from above. Just in time, they threw themselves further into the cave as the rumbling turned into a crash and their mouths and eyes were filled with dust. Spitting and coughing, they turned round to go back but it was too late. Moving the boulder had caused a roof-fall and now between them and the narrow entrance a mass of rocks completely blocked their way out. They were trapped.

As they stood there they heard Theo laugh. 'Well,' he

said. 'That's them shut up till we fancy moving it all to let them out. That's if we ever do let them out.'

'What do you mean?' said another voice.

'Well, what if we never move it? Wouldn't it save a lot of trouble if we told Charmides that his pet runaway had had an accident and got crushed to death? Think of the job we're going to have, fetching ropes and levers to heave these rocks out of the way. Why don't we just leave them to rot?'

There was a bit of muttering at that, but at last Theo said, 'All agreed then? We say they are dead.'

At that Phidias yelled, 'No. Don't leave us!' Before he could say more, however, they heard the men scrambling back down the cliff face and soon there was silence, broken only by the steady drip of water from the roof. It was pitch-black and icy cold.

Ari pulled her thin tunic round her. Her bare legs were cold aned scratched and she was very frightened. 'Phidias,' she said in a small voice, 'I'm, afraid. We shall have to stay here until we die. It's like Ulysses and his men when Polyphemus, the one-eyed giant, trapped them in a cave. Do you think there's a one-eyed giant in here?'

Phidias said, 'Of course not. And cheer up. They don't mean it. They're only trying to frighten us. Help will come soon.'

But as he looked again at the blocked entrance to the cave his heart sank and he said a silent prayer. 'Help us, Athena,' he breathed, silently so that Ari would not hear. 'Mighty Goddess Athena. Please help.'

CHAPTER FIVE

The Search

Early next morning, at Charmides' house, Theo and the other two servants went in to see their master who was eating breakfast, a flat scone of wheat bread and a piece of goat's cheese. He looked up and took a drink of honey and water from a terracotta cup. Then he wiped his mouth on a cloth and said, 'Well? Did you find her? Is she down at the slave market?'

Theo coughed nervously and said, 'Well, yes and no, Master.'

'What do you mean, idiot?' snapped Charmides.

Theo had rehearsed his story well. He glanced shiftily at his two companions and then rattled it off. 'Well, it was like this, master. We found her house all right, but then a great gang of men came out and attacked us with clubs. We fought bravely, but while we were doing that, Naxa and a man, her sister's husband we think, came out and ran off. We beat off our attackers and followed, but they had a good start and climbed up into a cave on the south side of the Acropolis.'

One of the others said, 'That's right. They climbed ever so far up. Quite small they looked to us, down below, so small that we weren't even sure that it was them.'

'It couldn't have been anybody else,' said Theo quickly, scowling at his companion. His eyes wandered round the room, not meeting those of his master. 'Anyway,' he went on. 'We knew it was them because we'd had them in sight right from when they left the house. So there they were, up in a cave, but we didn't like to follow too close, because rocks were falling off the cliff-face, and the damage the Persian army did, curse them, has made it very unsafe.'

'Never mind the Persians,' said Charmides. 'What happened?'

'Well, as I say, they had just crammed themselves into this sort of cave in the cliff when the rocks started to shake and when we looked again it had gone.'

'Gone? What had gone?'

'The cave entrance, Master. Disappeared. Blocked by great big boulders.'

'So what did you do? Don't tell me you just left them there?'

'Oh, no, Master. We risked our lives climbing up that cliff and trying to get in, but huge boulders blocked the way.'

'So?'

'We called out but there was no answer. Then we saw something horrible, Master, their legs sticking out from under massive rocks which had fallen on top of them. They were both crushed.'

Charmides stood up. 'Crushed? Are they dead?'

'Oh, yes, Master. Dead. Certainly. Nobody could live with that on top of them. Not even Hercules could have held up that lot.'

'That's terrible. I did not mean her to die,' said Charmides. 'We must go and get the bodies.'

The slave went pale. 'No use, Master. I haven't finished. Listen, hardly had we managed to get back to the ground ourselves, when there was another cliff fall and the whole place was covered in. We'll never be able to find it again.'

The other two shook their heads. 'No, never,' said one. 'It was so dark.'

Charmides sighed. There was something about the men's story that didn't ring true but there seemed to be little that he could do. In a way he had been fond of Naxa and had decided to go down to the slave market and fetch her back before she could be sold. Certainly he had not wished for her death. Added to that he knew his wife Hebe would be upset at the loss of her best nursemaid.

He frowned, then said, 'Oh, well, I suppose you did your best. Go your ways.'

The men shuffled out, glad to be away, and Charmides returned to his breakfast. He had hardly begun again, however, when there was a cry from up above and the sound of running feet. Seconds later Hebe burst into the room, followed by two servants.

'Charmides, I'm worried,' she said. 'I can't find the children and nobody seems to have seen them.'

'What next?' said Charmides angrily, but Hebe was so worried that he called all the servants together and sent them off to search. Outside, the streets were busy but Charmides himself, remembering his talk with Phidias, went down to seek out the metalworker Solon. He found him in his forge, red-faced from his work, and just fetching another bronze discus thrower out of its mould.

'Ha!' said Charmides. 'You. Solon. My son is missing. Have you seen him?'

The smith stroked his beard and looked him straight in the eyes. 'I have not, sir. At least I've not seen him today, but since you know my name you probably also know that he has been here a time or two.'

Charmides scowled. 'I know everything, and if he has come to harm because of you I'll have the skin flogged off your back.'

Solon knew better than to get angry at the harsh words. He shook his head. 'If I knew where he was, Master, I would tell you. All I know is that yesterday he took one of my models and said that he was going to draw out a better figure, one that looked more like an athlete.' He shook his head again. 'I pray to the gods that he has come to no harm. A likely lad, that, and could be a great sculptor.'

'Great rubbish!' snapped Charmides. 'I'll have no sculptors in my family. He's a citizen of Athens and possibly an Olympic athlete, not one of your back-street scoundrels.'

Solon shrugged. 'Then it will be Athens' loss,' he said. 'The boy has talent.'

By the time Charmides got back to the house, servants had been all over the city searching for the two missing children. Crassus at the Gymnasium had not seen them.

They had not been down to the theatre to see the players preparing for the latest play. They had not called on their friends. Ari's toys and her dolls were all in their place. Phidias's pet mice were in their cage and the grasshoppers the children had found the day before in the garden, were chirruping in a little wooden box.

'Lost!' said Charmides, taking the grasshoppers and releasing them. 'I can think of nowhere else to look.' He prowled around the house, then stopped by Phidias' bed. There, painted on the white wall was a sketch of an athlete, a discus held in the palm of his hand, arm back to throw and body tensed. Every muscle in the drawing told of the athlete's skill and Charmides could not help but admire it. It was a magnificent drawing. Perhaps after all he had been wrong about his son's wish to be a sculptor, but surely the boy would not run away, and take his sister with him, just because of that?

He looked round for the statue which Solon had mentioned but could not see it.

Meanwhile, upstairs Hebe wandered into the small store-room and saw the open window and Ari's spinning wheel with its spindle hanging down, empty of thread.

She called out, 'Charmides! Come up here. I think they might have climbed out of the window.'

Suddenly Charmides knew. 'Of course!' he shouted. 'How stupid of me not to think of it. They were fond of that wretched slave Naxa, the one who got crushed on the cliffs of the Acropolis. Do you think they went after her?'

He paused. Hebe who had not heard the news about her

favourite slave, cried out but Charmides hardly heard her. He was remembering again the shifty look on the faces of the men that morning. There was something odd about their story, something wrong with it.

It was peculiar, he thought, that one of the men had talked about the night being so dark, while their leader had spoken of being able to recognise people a long way off. And then what had that one man said? 'They seemed so small that we weren't even sure that it was them.' Apart from that, how could they have run so fast if the man was Naxa's brother-in-law, the one with the crippled leg?

As he stood, there was a noise outside and a man with a black beard hobbled in.

'Yes? What is it?' said Charmides, his thoughts still on the story of the cave.

'Master, my name is Zeno, married to the sister of your slave, Naxa.'

Charmides was across the room in one bound, seizing the man roughly and forcing him to his knees. 'What? I heard you were dead. Where is Naxa then? Is she dead or alive? What about my children?'

Another voice said, 'Master!' And there was Naxa, also on her knees, begging for mercy. 'Forgive me, Master,' she said tremblingly. 'I have been hiding outside till now, afraid to come in, but Zeno here just met one of your servants who told him that the children are missing. Oh, it's all my fault. They did it to save me from the slave market.'

Charmides turned to strike her, but Hebe pulled her to

her feet and said gently, 'Go to the baby, Naxa. I'll talk to you later. Charmides, this man may know where the children are. Let him speak.'

Zeno struggled to his feet. 'Forgive us, Charmides. Your children, those brave ones, led your slaves away from our house last night. I tried to stop them, but I am crippled and they are fleet of foot.

'And was that the last you saw of them?' said Charmides, a terrible thought coming into his head.

'Yes, Master, except that I know that they set off towards the Acropolis with your slaves after them.'

Charmides released his hold on the man. 'Oh ye gods!' he said. 'Then the two who were up on the cliffs, must have been Ari and Phidias. Oh, Athena, mighty goddess, may it not be so. Have mercy, let them not be dead.'

Then he roared, 'Send Theo to me! There are things I want to ask him.'

CHAPTER SIX

The Discus Thrower

'Is it daytime?' Ari opened her eyes and shivered as she felt the dampness of the cave floor seeping through her clothes. 'I've been asleep. How long have we been here?'

Phidias said, 'I don't know, several hours, I guess. A little light is coming through between the rocks at the entrance, but that may be the moon.'

'I'm hungry,' said Ari. 'How long will it be before Father comes?'

'Not long now,' said Phidias. 'He'll be getting a search party going.'

But in his heart he wondered whether a search party could ever find them. There were hundreds of cave entrances in the south face of the Acropolis and they all looked alike. How long would it take to search them all?

'I've nothing to eat,' he said. 'But if you're thirsty there are little puddles of water in the rocks. See.' He cupped his hands and drank from a pool which glistened faintly in the light seeping in from the entrance. It tasted bitter and very cold, but it was refreshing and he took some more.

Ari drank a little but made a face as she did so. 'Ugh. Horrid,' she said. 'What shall we do while we wait?'

Phidias said, 'Well, we could tell each other stories. Or we could sing a song.'

'No,' said Ari. 'I want to do something that makes me move. I feel cold and I keep thinking I can hear Polyphemus the giant.'

Phidias stood up and reached his hand above his head to touch the roof. He turned and strained his eyes to see further into the cave, but it was very dark. That gave him an idea.

'Look,' he said. 'We can't shift those big rocks, but we could move some of the rubble round them to let in more light.'

They scrabbled in the dust, pushing the rubble behind them and as they did so more light came into the cave. After a while they paused to shout for help, keeping it up for quite a long time, until at last they got tired and gave up.

It was now much lighter. 'Look,' said Ari and pointed. 'The cave goes further in. Let's explore.'

Phidias was doubtful. 'What if rescue comes while we are out of sight?' he said.

Ari said, 'We shall hear them. They're not going to shift those rocks without making a noise.'

Phidias said, 'The further in we go, the darker it will get. We might lose our way and never get back again.'

'That's true,' said Ari. 'No, wait a minute, I've got an idea. Look, when we left home I brought this.' She fished out the reel of thread which she had snatched from her spinning wheel. 'Do you remember the story of Theseus and how Princess Ariadne gave him some thread to trail behind him as he went into the labyrinth? So to find his way out again after he had killed the Minotaur, all he had to do was follow the thread. We could do the same. After all, my name is Ariadne, same as the Princess.'

She tied one end of the thread to a piece of broken stalactite and wedged it in the rocks at the entrance, then taking the thread in her hand, she started to walk into the darkness at the back of the cave.

'Come on,' she called. 'There's a tunnel going upwards, but we can climb.'

Phidias followed and looked up. The cave had turned into a rough-sided tunnel, sloping steeply upwards, almost like a wide chimney.

'You go first,' he said. 'Then if you start to fall I can support you. Give me the thread.'

They climbed slowly into the darkness, holding on to the sides and digging in their toes. As they climbed their eyes got used to the darkness so that the little light from below them was enough to see where they were going.

Soon the tunnel divided into two. 'Which way?' said Ari.

Phidias chose the tunnel that sloped more steeply and they went on. It divided again, so again they had to make a choice. It was very dark now so they chose the wider tunnel, feeling their way blindly along the walls.

The tunnel divided again and then still again. Each time the passageway got narrower and narrower and the air got poorer. Then at last Ari said, 'Look! Light!'

Ahead of them was a pale glow and this put new strength

into them so that they climbed rapidly, Phidias paying out the thread as they did so. A puff of fresh air in their faces felt cool.

'We must have come miles,' said Ari, pausing for breath. 'How much thread is left?'

'Not a lot,' said Phidias. 'If we don't find a way out soon we shall have to go back. I wouldn't like to get lost in this labyrinth.'

'Don't mention that word,' shivered Ari. 'I'm still thinking of Theseus and the Minotaur. Was there really such a beast, do you think?'

'Go on,' said Phidias and then suddenly they found themselves crawling up through a narrow opening to stand in a cave once more. But the roof of this one was very high above them, its towering walls too steep to climb, its floor littered with soil and rocks. Massive stalagmites rose from the ground and high above them milky water dripped from long stalactites.

But Ari and Phidias didn't mind the water. Their eyes were fixed on something else up in the roof, for up there was was a hole, big enough for a man to squeeze through, and round the edges of the hole they could see grass and above that was blue sky.

'We've made it!' shouted Ari. 'Daylight!' She jumped up and down in excitement but then came disaster, because as she landed she caught her foot on a sharp rock and fell, twisting her leg. 'Ouch,' she said. 'That hurt.'

Phidias was looking up at the cliff-like walls. He shook his head and said, 'We've not made it, not really. We can't climb these walls, so we can't get out of there. Come on, let's go back, the sooner we get to the entrance again the better.'

But Ari was sitting holding her ankle. 'Sorry,' she said, with a brave smile, 'but I think I've pulled a muscle or something. I shall never get all the way down there again.'

Phidias took a look. His sister's ankle was swelling rapidly and it was clear that she could not walk on it. 'I don't think it's broken,' he said, 'but we really can't stay here in case rescuers are already down below. Will you wait here while I go back to the cave entrance and look?'

'No, don't leave me. What if Polyphemus comes with his one eye? Suppose the Minotaur is waiting in the dark?'

Phidias snapped, 'Your head's full of stories. What's happened to that girl who wanted to do what boys do? There's no such thing as a Minotaur. All you've got to do is wait.'

'On my own?' said Ari. 'It's wet and I'm cold and I shall die if you leave me, so there.'

Phidias looked up at the roof of the cave again. Perhaps there was a way to get out up there after all. The hole was certainly big enough for a man to get through, but the sides of the cave were too steep to climb. What could be done?

He looked up again, and as he looked the sun must have come from behind a cloud. A pillar of light, hung with specks of floating dust, struck down through the hole like a flash of lightning, making him cover his eyes and gasp. As he did so he heard Ari call out.

'Look,' she said. 'There's somebody up there.'

Phidias shaded his eyes against the sun's beam, but the light was so strong that it was difficult to look for long. Was there somebody? He blinked and wiped his watering eyes. There did seem to be a tall figure up there, possibly a woman, but what kind of woman wore a helmet and carried a sword and shield? He blinked again and the figure had gone.

'Who was it?' said Ari. 'Why didn't you call?'

'I don't know. The light was so strong. I thought I saw somebody. There was an owl screeching up there as well.'

'It looked like a woman.'

'Could have been.'

'I thought I saw a helmet and a shield. Did you say you heard an owl?' Ari was very excited.

Phidias said, 'Now, don't let's be silly. You're not thinking what I'm thinking, are you?'

'Yes,' came the answer. 'Back there I said a little prayer to the goddess Athena for help and I think she has come to rescue us.'

'You're crazy,' said Phidias. 'Nobody's ever seen her.'

'Theseus did. And Ulysses did.'

'Stories again?' said Phidias.

Ari said, 'Theseus wasn't a story. They've just brought

his bones back to Athens, so how could he be just a story? There is a goddess Athena and I know she has come to help us. The owl proves it. There's always an owl about when she's near.'

Phidias was not convinced. He squatted down on his heels to think and as he did so he felt something sharp dig into him. It was the little figure of a discus thrower, still in the leather bag on his belt. It gave him an idea and he fished it out.

'Listen,' he said. 'I've had a thought. Whoever that was we know for certain that it's daylight up there, so we know more or less where we are. We've climbed and scrambled quite a way and all the time it's been uphill. The roof is now only about fifty feet up, so I'm pretty sure that up there is the flat top of the Acropolis.'

'So what? Fifty feet is fifty feet. I've hurt my ankle and we're still stuck.'

Phidias bent down again. 'It's too high to jump out, but it's not too high to throw something out. Look.' He showed her the litle statue.

Ari said, 'You think that if you throw it up there someone will see it?'

'Not only see it, but come over to pick it up. Then they will hear our yells and we shall be rescued.'

Ari said. 'It's a long way up and if you miss, it will fall back down and you'll lose it in the rubble.'

Phidias looked up. What he had to throw wasn't anything like the discus he used at the Gymnasium. A discus flew in a smooth curve and a good athlete could almost guarantee where it would land, but this little statue was an awkward shape. He had to throw it upwards through a small hole and the light was in his eyes, dazzling him. Added to that he was standing on rough, slippery rock and his fingers were sore from the climbing.

But it was worth a try, so he narrowed his eyes, murmured, 'Help me, Athena,' curved his body and threw with all his strength.

The little statue flew like a golden bird up, up and then straight through the hole and out into the sunlight. Ari cheered, and Phidias said, 'That's right. Shout for help. Shout!'

Their wailing voices seemed tiny in the vast cave, but they kept on calling for a long time until at last Phidias sighed and said, 'Give it a rest. We'll try again later. Somebody is bound to see the statue.'

Ari said, 'I'm cold, I'm tired and my ankle hurts. But I won't cry. I'll be brave and strong. Oh, Athena, why don't you come to our aid?'

CHAPTER SEVEN

The Woman

Charmides looked up at the cliff. With him were Theo and the other two slaves, together with eight or nine strong men, all carrying tools and ropes.

'Where was this cave?' said Charmides angrily.

Theo rubbed his bristly chin. 'Up there somewhere, master. It was dark. Perhaps that one, or, no, it could have been that one there. But then that other one looks like it as well.'

'Idiot!' said Charmides. 'Think, man, there must be something to tell you which one. You may yet save yourself a flogging.'

They looked but there was nothing to help them. The cliff face seemed to be riddled with fissures and cave entrances, so it was obvious they were going to have a long search.

'And are you sure they were crushed by the rocks?' said Charmides. 'You'd better tell me the truth. Those were my children up there.'

Theo stammered. 'Well, we didn't actually see them crushed. I thought I saw their feet under the rock, but it could have been some bits of wood.'

'You wouldn't know the truth if you met it in the street,' snarled Charmides. 'Here, you men, we'll waste no more time. Start at the nearest cave and climb up to each one in turn.'

The first man had just set his hands to the rocks, however, when an owl screeched and flew like a bullet over their heads, up to the top of the cliffs and out of sight. As they turned to watch it, they were surprised to see what looked like an old woman in poor clothing. She was standing, balanced on the cliff high above them, holding her hands up to the sky and chanting. The sun was behind her and it was as if she were bathed in a golden light.

'Who's that? What's she saying?' said Charmides, squinting into the bright light.

There was a shout and Zeno came hobbling up. He too was pointing up at the old woman on the cliff. 'Have you seen her, master? She is shouting a prayer of thanks to the gods, who have sent her a gift.'

'What gift?' said Charmides. He shaded his eyes and shouted up to the woman, 'What gift?'

She held up something which glistened in the sun. 'A statue of an athlete, my masters!' she called in a shrill, wailing voice. 'Give glory to the gods, for they have sent me this golden gift.'

Charmides shrugged and turned back to his slaves. 'There's all sorts of rubble up there,' he said. 'Bits and pieces from the old temple of Athena. Forget her, she's mad.' He turned to Zeno. 'Where have you come from?' he said. 'Have you any news?'

'No, master. I went home, where our child is well again and will live. And there was a message that I have my job back at the docks. All thanks to Phidias and Ari, so I came to see if I could help in the search.'

Charmides nodded his thanks, and then suddenly remembered something. He turned his face up again and shouted to the woman on the cliffs, 'An athlete, did you say? What kind of an athlete?'

The woman held up the figure again. 'A beautiful statue. See, it is a man throwing the discus.'

Charmides' heart gave a bump. 'A discus thrower, did you say?' He remembered the drawing by the bed and he remembered the words of Solon the metal worker.

'Where did you say it came from?' he called.

The woman seemed to shimmer in the sun and her words were almost lost in the breeze. 'The gods sent it to me, back there, in the ruins. I know it was from the gods bcause I could hear them singing and calling to me from beneath my feet.'

'Master,' said Zeno. I know this hillside. It's riddled with grottoes and fissures, so it's possible that a cave or a pothole runs right up to the top.'

'Right, you stay here with me,' said Charmides. 'Some of the rest of you take ropes and climb up to the woman, and when you get up there put your ears to the ground to listen.'

A group of men attacked the cliffs and were soon at the top while Charmides scanned the rock face. Some way below where the woman had stood he spotted a place where there seemed to have been a fresh fall of rock. 'Could that be the cave?' he said to Theo.

Theo said, 'Yes, it could have been, but it was dark, Master.'

Zeno, in spite of his leg, scrambled up. 'It looks like a cave,' he called excitedly, 'but it's blocked by rocks. Wait! Master, see, there's a bit of thread poking through a hole!'

'That's it!' said Charmides excitedly. 'Hebe said some wool was missing from Ari's spinning wheel.'

It took some time to lever the huge rocks out of the way, but at last the cave entrance was clear and there on the floor was a golden thread running back into the darkness.

'Follow me,' said Charmides. 'There's hope yet.' He picked up the thread and began to climb, the rest scrambling after him, squeezing along the narrow passageways. Each time there was a choice of tunnels the thread told them which one to take. Then suddenly there was a cry ahead.

'Help!' said a voice and seconds later Charmides had his arms round his son while Ari sat holding her swollen ankle. Charmides listened to their story, looking grimly at Theo when the children told of their escape from the house of the blue dolphin.

'Your punishment will come later,' he said to the frightened slave. 'But for now, just be thankful that we got here in time.'

Far above them there was a shout and there, looking down through the hole, were the men Charmides had sent up to the top.

'Let down a rope,' shouted Charmides. 'Ari, we'll make a loop and you can sit in it to be pulled up. Phidias and I will go up too. Zeno, you come last. The rest of can go back the way we came.'

It took very little time to haul them out of the cave and Charmides looked round for the old woman. Funnily enough, the statue of the discus thrower was lying nearby but of her there was no trace. Charmides could not understand it. 'Why did she drop the statue? Is nobody here?' he shouted to the men.

'Nobody, Master, one called. 'But there's something curious over here where the old Temple of Athena once stood. Look.'

On the ground lay heaps of rubble, broken sculptures and fallen columns. In one open space was a huge chunk of stone, carved to represent a battle between gods and giants. In front of it the dust was fine and smooth, and there they could see the outlines of something round and something long.

Ari hobbled over, 'I knew it was Athena,' she said triumphantly. 'That will be where she rested her sword and shield.'

Phidias was about to scoff when she bent down and picked something up. 'And look,' she said, hardly daring to breathe in excitement. 'Look at this!'

She held out her hand to show a tiny stone mouse, perfectly formed down to the last whisker.

Charmides remembered Athena's shield, on which hung the head of the gorgon Medusa, that head that turned everything into stone. Here was a stone mouse, close by where someone had rested something, perhaps a

measuring pole and a bucket. Or could it really have been a spear and a shield?

He spoke softly. 'Phidias. Ari. You were foolish but I believe the gods smile on those who take risks for others. And those the gods smile on deserve rewards, so you, Phidias, may learn that craft of casting bronze from your old metic, Solon. Later on, after the Olympic Games, I may let you work alongside a true sculptor, perhaps even the great Myron.'

Phidias was overjoyed. 'Thank you, Father' he said. 'And one day, I will raise a beautiful statue to the goddess Athena, to stand above the cave near to where the discus thrower landed. It will be such a wonderful statue that men will come from all over the world to see it and to marvel at the glory of Athens and its great sculptors.'

'Great show-offs,' said Ari. 'And what about me? What will be my reward?'

'Well,' said Charmides. 'Naxa can come back to the house, so you will be able to tell her stories instead of the other way round. And since, like your namesake Ariadne, your golden thread led us through the cave, I'll have a new spinning wheel made for you'

Ari pulled a face and said, 'No, thank you. Oh, wait, on the other hand that might not be such a bad idea. I could weave myself a boy's tunic, dress in it and see if I can persuade those dunderheads at the Gymnasium to let me join in the athletics. Then I can learn to throw things like Phidias.'

They turned for home and as they did so the owl, perched high on a ruined pillar above the Acropolis, spread its wings, lowered its head and watched them go.

PLACES TO VISIT

Relics of Ancient Greek civilisation may be found at the following museums, though in some cases the exhibits are limited in scope. Some museums offer an education service or guided tours. An information-seeking telephone call is therefore recommended.

ABERDEEN University Marischal Museum	0224–273131
BIRMINGHAM Museum & Art Gallery	021–235–2834
CAMBRIDGE University Museum of Classical Archeology	0223–335153
CARDIFF National Museum of Wales	0222–397951
EXETER Royal Albert Museum & Art Gallery	0392–265858
LONDON British Museum	071–636–1555
MACCLESFIELD West Park Museum	0625–619831
MANCHESTER University Museum	061–275–2634
NEWCASTLE UPON TYNE Greek Museum	091–2226000
NOTTINGHAM Castle Museum	0602–483504
OXFORD Ashmolean Museum of Art & Archaeology	0865–278000
PORT SUNLIGHT Lady Lever Art Gallery	051–207–0001
READING Ure Museum of Greek Archeology	0734–318420
SHEFFIELD City Museum	0742–768588
WELLS NEXT THE SEA Holkham Hall	0328–710227